THE CAT IN THE HAT COMES BACK!

By Dr. Seuss

This edition produced for The Book People Ltd,
Hall Wood Avenue, Haydock, St Helens WA11 9UL

Trademark Random House Inc.
Authorised user HarperCollins *Publishers* Ltd

4 6 8 10 9 7 5 3

ISBN 0 583 32417 7

A Beginner Book published by arrangement with
Random House Inc., New York, USA
First published in the UK 1961

Printed and bound in Hong Kong

This was no time for play.

This was no time for fun.

This was no time for games.

There was work to be done.

All that deep,

Deep, deep snow,

All that snow had to go.

When our mother went
Down to the town for the day,
She said, "Somebody has to
Clean all this away.
Somebody, SOMEBODY
Has to, you see."
Then she picked out two Somebodies.
Sally and me.

Well . . .

There we were.

We were working like that

And then who should come up

But the CAT IN THE HAT!

"Oh-oh!" Sally said.

"Don't you talk to that cat.

That cat is a bad one,

That Cat in the Hat.

He plays lots of bad tricks.

Don't you let him come near.

You know what he did

The last time he was here."

"Play tricks?" laughed the cat.
"Oh, my my! No, no, no!
I just want to go in
To get out of the snow.
Keep your mind on your work.
You just stay there, you two.
I will go in the house
And find something to do."

Then that cat went right in!

He was up to no good!

So I ran in after

As fast as I could!

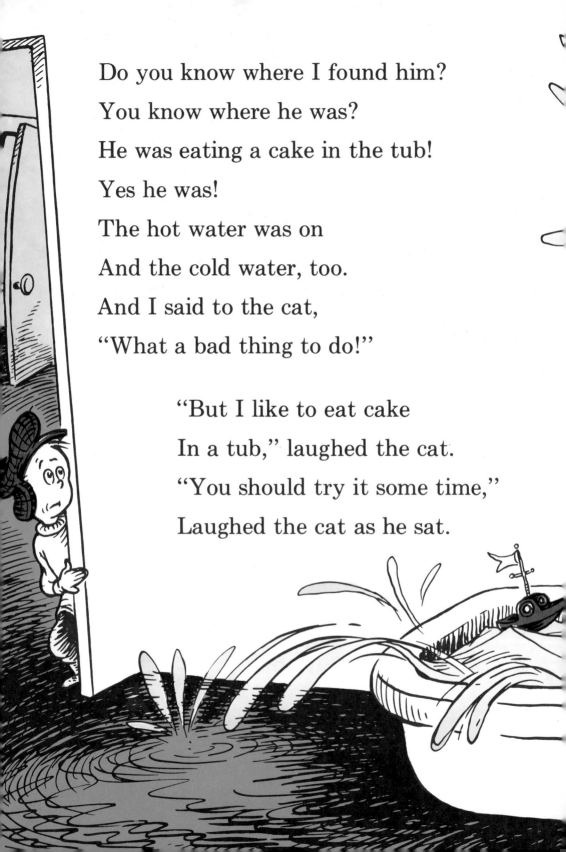

Do you know where I found him?

You know where he was?

He was eating a cake in the tub!

Yes he was!

The hot water was on

And the cold water, too.

And I said to the cat,

"What a bad thing to do!"

"But I like to eat cake

In a tub," laughed the cat.

"You should try it some time,"

Laughed the cat as he sat.

And then I got mad.
This was no time for fun.
I said, "Cat! You get out!
There is work to be done.
I have no time for tricks.
I must go back and dig.
I can't have you in here
Eating cake like a pig!
You get out of this house!
We don't want you about!"
Then I shut off the water
And let it run out.

The water ran out.
And then I saw the ring!
A ring in the tub!
And, oh boy! What a thing!
A big long pink cat ring!
It looked like pink ink!
And I said, "Will this ever
Come off? I don't think!"

"Have no fear of that ring,"
Laughed the Cat in the Hat.
"Why, I can take cat rings
Off tubs. Just like that!"

Do you know how he did it?
WITH MOTHER'S WHITE DRESS!
Now the tub was all clean,
But her dress was a mess!

Then Sally looked in.
Sally saw the dress, too!
And Sally and I
Did not know what to do.
We should work in the snow.
But that dress! What a spot!
"It may never come off!"
Sally said. "It may not!"

But the cat laughed, "Ho! Ho!
I can make the spot go.
The way I take spots off a dress
Is just so!"

"See here!" laughed the cat.

"It is not hard at all.

The thing that takes spots

Off a dress is a wall!"

Then we saw the cat wipe

The spot off the dress.

Now the dress was all clean.

But the wall! What a mess!

"Oh, wall spots!" he laughed.
"Let me tell you some news.
To take spots off a wall,
All I need is two shoes!"

Whose shoes did he use?
I looked and saw whose!
And I said to the cat,
"This is very bad news.
Now the spot is all over
DAD'S £7 SHOES!"

"But your dad will not
Know about that,"
Said the cat.
"He will never find out,"
Laughed the Cat in the Hat.
"His £7 shoes will have
No spots at all.
I will rub them right off
On this rug in the hall."

"But now we have rug spots!"
I yelled. "What a day!
Rug spots! What next?
Can you take THEM away?"

"Don't ask me," he laughed.
"Why, you know that I can!"
Then he picked up the rug
And away the cat ran.

26

"I can clean up these rug spots
Before you count three!
No spots are too hard
For a Hat Cat like me!"

He ran into Dad's bedroom
And then the cat said,
"It is good that your dad
Has the right kind of bed."

Then he shook the rug!
CRACK!
Now the bed had the spot!
And all I could say was,
"Now what, Cat?
NOW what?"

But the cat just stood still.

He just looked at the bed.

"This is NOT the right kind of a bed,"

The cat said.

"To take spots off THIS bed

Will be hard," said the cat.

"I can't do it alone,"

Said the Cat in the Hat.

"It is good I have some one
To help me," he said.
"Right here in my hat
On the top of my head!
It is good that I have him
Here with me today.
He helps me a lot.
This is Little Cat A."

And then Little Cat A
Took the hat off HIS head.
"It is good I have some one
To help ME," he said.
"This is Little Cat B.
And I keep him about,
And when I need help
Then I let him come out."

And then B said,

"I think we need Little Cat C.

That spot is too much ·

For the A cat and me.

But now, have no fear!

We will clean it away!

The three of us! Little Cats B, C and A!"

"Come on! Take it away!"
Yelled Little Cat A.

"I will hit that old spot
With this broom! Do you see?
It comes off the old bed!
It goes on the T.V."

And then Little Cat B
Cleaned up the T.V.

He cleaned it with milk,
Put the spot in a pan!
And then C blew it out
Of the house with a fan!

39

"But look where it went!"
I said. "Look where it blew!
You blew the mess
Out of the house. That is true.
But now you made Snow Spots!
You can't let THEM stay!"

"Let us think about that now,"
Said C, B and A.

"With some help, we can do it!"
Said Little Cat C.
Then POP! On his head
We saw Little Cat D!
Then, POP! POP! POP!
Little Cats E, F and G!

"We will clean up that snow
If it takes us all day!
If it takes us all night,
We will clean it away!"
Said Little Cats G, F, E, D, C, B, A.

They ran out of the house then
And we ran out, too.
And the Big Cat laughed,
"Now you will see something new!
My cats are all clever.
My cats are good shots.
My cats have good guns.
They will kill all those spots!"

But this did not look
Very clever to me.
Kill snow spots with pop guns?
That just could not be!

"All this does is make MORE spots!"

We yelled at the cat.

"Your cats are no good.

Put them back in your hat.

46

"Take your Little Cats G,
F, E, D, C, B, A.
Put them back in your hat
And you take them away!"

"Oh, no!" said the cat.
"All they need is more help.
Help is all that they need.
So keep still and don't yelp."

Then Little Cat G
Took the hat off his head.
"I have Little Cat H
Here to help us," he said.

"Little Cats H, I, J,
K, L and M.
But our work is so hard
We must have more than them.
We need Little Cat N.
We need O. We need P.
We need Little Cats Q, R, S, T,
U and V."

"Come on! Kill those spots!

Kill the mess!" yelled the cats.

And they jumped at the snow

With long rakes and red bats.

They put it in pails

And they made high pink hills!

Pink snow men! Pink snow balls!

And little pink pills!

Oh, the things that they did!
And they did them so hard,
It was all one big spot now
All over the yard!
But the Big Cat stood there
And he said, "This is good.
This is what they should do
And I knew that they would.

"With a little more help,
All the work will be done.
They need one more cat.
And I know just the one."

"Look close! In my hand
I have Little Cat V.
On his head are Cats W,
X, Y and Z."

"Z is too small to see.
So don't try. You can not.
But Z is the cat
Who will clean up that spot!"

"Now here is the Z
You can't see," said the Cat.
"And I bet you can't guess
What he has in HIS hat!

"He has something called VOOM.
Voom is so hard to get,
You never saw anything
Like it, I bet.
Why, Voom cleans up anything
Clean as can be!"
Then he yelled,
"Take your hat off now,
Little Cat Z!
Take the Voom off your head!
Make it clean up the snow!
Hurry! You Little Cat!
One! Two! Three! GO!"

Then the Voom . . .

It went VOOM!

And, oh boy! What a VOOM!

Now, don't ask me what Voom is.

I never will know.

But, boy! Let me tell you

It DOES clean up snow!

"So you see!" laughed the Cat,

"Now your snow is all white!

Now your work is all done!

Now your house is all right!

And you know where my little cats are?"

Said the cat.

"That Voom blew my little cats

Back in my hat.

And so, if you ever

Have spots, now and then,

I will be very happy

To come here again . . .

"...with Little Cats A, B, C, D...

E, F, G...

H, I, J, K...

L, M, N...

and O, P .

and Q, R, S, T . . .

   and Cat U and Cat V . . .

      and Little Cats W

               X

                Y

            and Z!''